PUBLISHED BY
Red Robin Books Limited
Coppins Barn, Wearne, Langport,
Somerset TA10 0Q J, UK
www.redrobinbooks.com

ISBN: 978-1-908702-94-4

First published in the UK 2021

Editor – Francesca Pinagli
Design – David Rose
Printed by ADverts, Latvia

Nederlands
letterenfonds
**dutch foundation
for literature**

This publication has been made possible with financial
support from the Dutch Foundation for Literature.

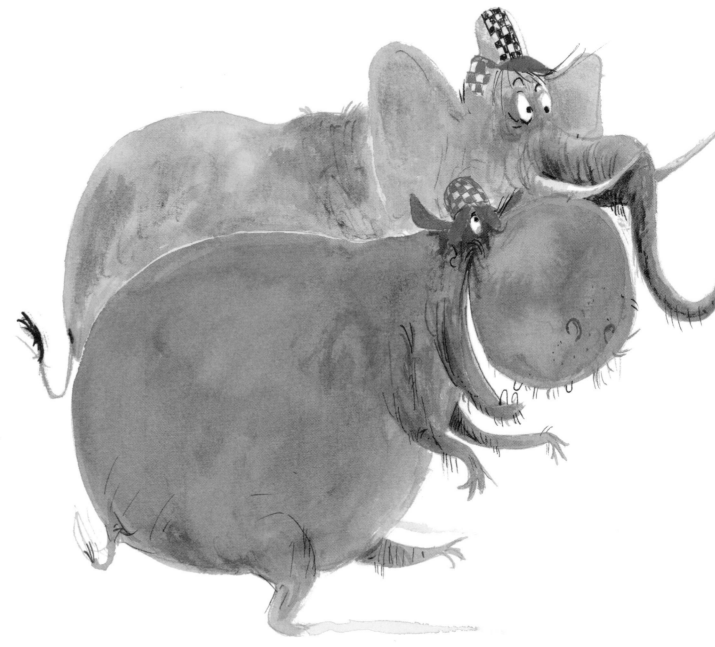

Robbie's Little Red Tractor

Harmen van Straaten

TRANSLATED BY
Laura Watkinson

An exciting race is about to begin!

And who do you think is going to win?

Hippo shouts, "GET OUT OF MY WAY!

I'm going to get the prize today!"

"HEY!" says Robbie. "Wait a minute!
I'm racing too – and I'm going to win it!
My tractor might not be that fast,
but I'll be first. And you'll be last!"

"Out of the way, we're coming through!"
squeal Piglet One and Piglet Two.
"Our terrific yellow truck
always brings us lots of luck.
The rest of you should just give up,
There's no way you'll win the cup!"

Robbie smiles...

"Piglets, piglets, please calm down.

My little red tractor is the best in town!"

Elephant trumpets, "Don't bother trying!
Soon I'll be cheering – and you'll be crying!
My bulldozer will push you clear away.
Why don't you go home and play?"

Robbie gulps...
"Really?" he says. "Well, I don't care.
My little red tractor will win. So there!"

"WAIT!" shouts Rhino. "I'm racing too!
Hey, Robbie! I'm revving up next to you.
You'd better not start in front of ME.
The best driver's going to win, you'll see!"
"That's right!" says Robbie, with a smile on his face.
"My little red tractor will take first place."

"Squeak!" comes a voice from down below.
It's little Mouse – and he's ready to go.
"My super-speedy clockwork car
will go really fast and really far."

The animals laugh…

"Mouse, by the time you finish the race,

We'll be home and feeling ace."

Here comes Tiger in his yellow digger.
"Here I am, chaps! I'm better and bigger!
I've not come here to spoil your fun,
but there is no doubt – I'M number one!

HA! Look at your vehicles in a line.

My digger's the best. The prize is mine!

Good luck to the lot of you.

You're really going to need it, too.

As for Robbie's little red tractor…

NO! It doesn't have the winning factor!"

The other animals all agree,
"Oh, why, Robbie, can't you see?
There's really no point you joining in.
Your little red tractor will never win!"
"Enough!" says Robbie. "The race can start,
And my little red tractor WILL take part."

"Alright, everyone, get set to go.

HEY, YOU! STOP THAT! NO! NO! NO!"

Sneaky Elephant's driving off already!

But now the rest can leave. Ready, steady...

GO!

"VROOOMMMMM...
BROOOMMMMM!"

the vehicles roar.

An animal race! Who could wish for more?

Which one's going to be the first?

Which one's going to drive the worst?

Which one's going to mess it up?

Which one's going to win the cup?

Rhino's police car soon gets stuck
between the fire engine and the yellow truck.

BOOMMMMM!

All three bump into Mouse's car,
which didn't go fast and didn't go far.
And because the animals make such a dash,
it all ends up in a massive...

CRASH!!!!!

"Why didn't you just let me past?"

"It's your fault that we're going to be last!"

"You've made us lose! What a shame!"

"Me?" squeaks Mouse. "No. YOU'RE to blame!"

Then, in the distance, there's a chugging sound.

It's Robbie's tractor – and it's gaining ground.

Robbie drives up to the site of the crash.

"The trophy's mine and I didn't dash!

You all lost because you were in such a hurry.

But no one's hurt, so there's no need to worry.

I'll tow you home in time for dinner.

Because my little red tractor...

is a GREAT BIG WINNER!"